A Pig and His Pet

Fulton Books, Inc.
Meadville, PA

Published by Fulton Books 2021

ISBN 978-1-63710-393-7 (paperback)
ISBN 978-1-63710-394-4 (digital)

Printed in the United States of America

A Pig and His Pet

Written by Cheryl Pappas

Pictures by Namal Designs

1

Sally lived with her parents and her big brother Jake on a nice big farm.

They lived in a red house. There was a big red barn next to their house and lots of room for all the animals that lived there too.

5

Sally loved living there because she could visit the animals every day and help take care of them.

Sally's family has many animals on the farm already. There are cows (*moo*) and sheep (*baa*).

And horses (*neigh*) and chickens (*cluck*).

They even have a pet dog (*woof*) and a cat (*meow*).

Sally has a job on the farm. She feeds the animals and makes sure they have plenty of water. Sometimes she lets them out, and she and her brother Jake run around and play with them to give them some exercise.

One day, Sally's parents came home with a very special animal, a little duck (*quack*).

Sally was asked to help take care of the duck, so she put it in the pigpen to keep it safe.

Perry was a cute little pig (*oink*), who lived in the pen and was so excited to see another animal come to visit him.

Sally's mom wasn't sure if putting the duck in with the pig was such a good idea. Sally asked if they could just give it some time to see if they got along.

Sally's mom agreed, and she put the duck in the pen with Perry.

Sally would wake up in the morning and go out to the pen and watch Perry and the duck now named Dahlia. Perry would nudge Dahlia over to the food to make sure she was eating.

Perry would nudge Dahlia to the big mud puddle to make sure she had a bath.

Then Perry would nudge Dahlia to the bale of hay to make sure she would take a nap. Sally saw Perry do this day in and day out. Dahlia and Perry seemed to get along very well.

When the other farm animals were put in the pen by Sally's brother Jake, Perry would hover over Dahlia to keep her safe and make sure the other animals would not harm her.

Perry would make sure that Dahlia had enough room to waddle around, and he would make sure she did not get squished by the other animals.

After a few months, Sally's parents thought that Dahlia the duck was getting too big for the pen, and they moved her to her own little coop.

Perry the Pig now seemed very sad. He would just lay in the pen and would not care about any of the other animals around him.

Every day, Sally went outside to make sure Dahlia was okay. She could see Dahlia looking at Perry in his pen. Dahlia stopped splashing in the water, she stopped eating, and she wouldn't lay down in her new bed of hay.

Poor Perry was so sad he would not go near his hay bed and would not eat his food.

Sally watched how sad Dahlia and Perry were for a few days. Then Sally went to talk to her mom. She told her how Perry and Dahlia both seemed so sad because they were not with each other. Sally's mom wondered what she should do. Sally begged her to put them back together in the same pen.

45

The next day, the whole family went outside and took Dahlia out of her coop and put her back in the pen with Perry.

Dahlia was so happy she quacked, and she spread her wings, and she ran around and around.

Perry was also very happy as he snuggled and nudged Dahlia. He oinked and splashed in the mud.

Sally was so happy to finally see her pig and his pet back together. The two would never be apart again.

About the Author

Cheryl Pappas is an entrepreneur that loves to dabble in songwriting, poetry, and painting. While running her own market research firm, she has always wanted to pursue writing. Her passion is to write children's books.